# Season Isle

TICK TOCK TREE

ROLY POLY HILL

TANGLE WOODS

BIG MOUNTAIN

SHADOW VALLEY

HIDE-AWAY CAVE

For my sister and personal cheerleader, Claire

First published in Great Britain 2022 by Farshore
An imprint of HarperCollins*Publishers*
1 London Bridge Street, London SE1 9GF
www.farshore.co.uk

HarperCollins*Publishers*
1st Floor, Watermarque Building, Ringsend Road
Dublin 4, Ireland

Text and illustrations copyright © Jo Lindley 2022

Jo Lindley has asserted her moral rights.

ISBN 978 0 7555 0341 4
Printed in the UK by a CarbonNeutral® company.
1

A CIP catalogue record for this title is available from the British Library.

MIX
Paper from
responsible sources
FSC™ C007454

This book is produced from independently certified FSC™ paper
to ensure responsible forest management.

For more information visit: www.harpercollins.co.uk/green

# Hello Spring

Jo Lindley

Spring and her three best friends **loved** playing together.

All year round, they took it in turns to wear the weather crown and lead the games.

For months, Winter had led the games. Her friends had enjoyed making snowballs, snow angels and sledging through the frozen forest.

But today was a very important day.

Today, Winter would hand the weather crown to Spring and a whole **new season** would begin.

As Winter placed the crown
on Spring's head, the sun
felt instantly warmer.

Already Spring was imagining
colourful flowers, dancing butterflies,
singing birds, and buzzing bees . . .

It was going to be the best, brightest
and most beautiful spring ever, she decided.

Winter had been amazing.
But spring would be . . . incredible!

They didn't have to wait long for the first flower
to pop up through the ground.

"It's going to be **SO** pretty,"
said Summer.

"I wonder what
colour it'll be?"
said Autumn.

They waited.

And **waited.**

"Why won't it open?" Spring frowned.

She was starting to feel anxious.

"Don't worry," said Summer.

"Let's wake the butterflies while we wait."

Spring tapped gently on
the butterflies' cocoons.
"Wakey-wakey," she called.
**"Time to dance."**

But the butterflies wouldn't
come out to show off their colours.
"What about the birds?"
suggested Summer.

Spring climbed up
to the nearest nest.
"Wakey-wakey," she said.
"Time to sing!"

But the birds were silent.

So were the frogs.
The bunnies were hiding away.
The bees weren't buzzing . . .

There wasn't a green leaf to be seen.

Spring crumpled to the ground with a sob.

"I don't understand!" she cried.

"Last time everything was . . . perfect!"

Her friends gathered close.

"I have an idea," said Winter. "We'll help!"

Spring watched as the seasons got to work . . .

Winter collected her
brightest paint.

Autumn sewed his cape into
butterfly wings.

And Summer chose
a choir of blackbirds.

Before long, the meadow was brimming with **vibrant colours** and **happy sounds.**

It was working!
The snow had started to melt and
Spring felt her heart growing lighter.

But at that moment . . .

**BOOOOOM!**

a crack of thunder ripped through the stormy clouds above.

It startled Summer's birds,

who flew off with Autumn's wings,

spilling Winter's paint
**everywhere.**

And then . . .

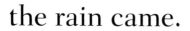
the rain came.

The seasons watched
as the smile fell from
Spring's face.

"Oops!" gulped Autumn.
"What a **mess!**"

But suddenly Spring let out a giggle.
"We . . . look . . . so . . . **silly**," she gasped.

The giggle became a roar of **laughter** and soon
her friends were laughing too.

And Spring realised no season
needed to be **perfect!** It didn't matter
if spring was messy or soggy
as long as it was **fun!**

"I think I'm ready to try again!"
she smiled.

She closed her eyes. With each breath, she imagined the scent of her favourite flower until a single delicate buttercup floated into view.

"I see it!" beamed Spring, "and it's yellow!"

Her friends
huddled closer and
the grey clouds
floated away.

"Keep going!"
encouraged Summer.
"We believe in you," declared Winter.

Spring pictured fresh green leaves swaying in the breeze,

vibrant flowers reaching up towards the sun,

butterflies flitting and birds swooping,

a dazzling symphony of colours.

"Oh!" gasped her friends. "It's magical!"

Spring could feel herself bursting with joy.
But it wasn't because of the dazzling butterflies or
the shimmering leaves or the chirruping birds.

"There's only one thing that **really**
matters," she told them . . .

"my friends!"

# Season Isle

TICK
TOCK
TREE

ROLY POLY HILL

TANGLE WOODS

BIG
MOUNTAIN

SHADOW VALLEY

HIDE-AWAY
CAVE